Little Frog and the

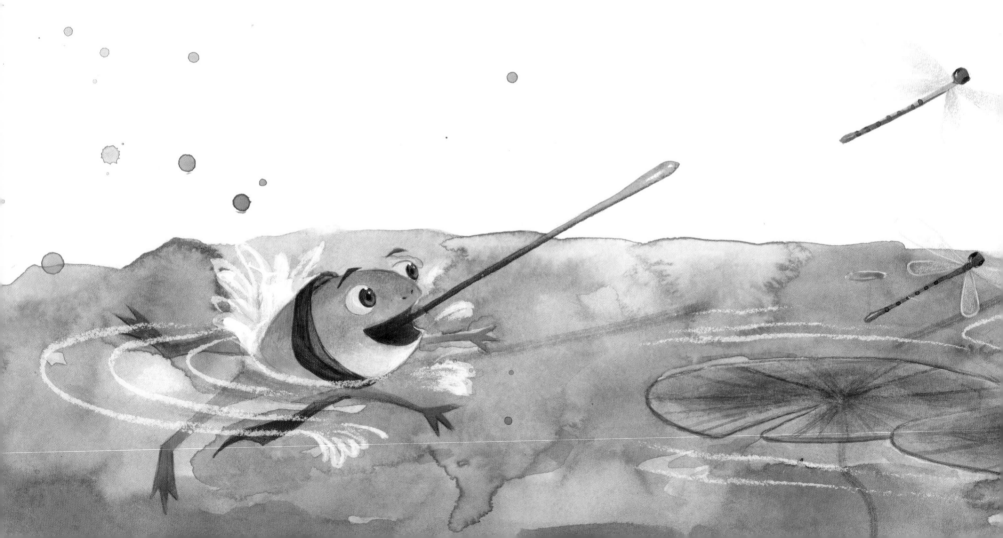

Scary Autumn Thing

Story by Jane Yolen   Illustrated by Ellen Shi

PERSNICKETY PRESS

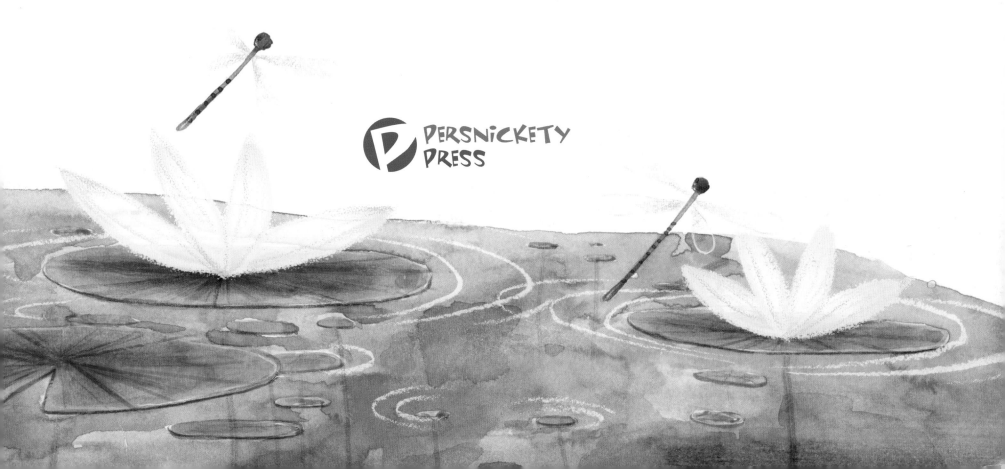

To Elizabeth H. and her
mischief of boys.

—J. Y.

To Greg and Fred, my first
froggy friends.

—E. S.

Text copyright © 2016 by Jane Yolen
Illustrations copyright © 2016 by Ellen Shi

Designed by Hans Teensma, Impress

Published by Persnickety Press

ISBN 978-1943978-01-4

CPSIA Tracking Label Information
Production Location: Guangdong, China
Production Date: 5/1/2016
Cohort: Batch 1
Batch Number: 66461-0

Frogs love green:
green water,
green lily pads,
green leaves.
Green!

But autumn had come to The Pond,
turning everything red and gold.
To Little Frog, red and gold were scary.
They were the colors of hot sun and cold blood.
She sat on a green lily pad,
and contemplated the trees.
Half of them were now yellow.
Two of them were orange.
One was a bright red.
All the rest were still green.
Sort of.

She had never seen such a thing before.
(Well, she was only a *Little* Frog,
and it *was* her first Fall.)
Little Frog shuddered.

Mama Frog jumped up next to her
which made the lily pad sway.
Little Frog usually loved such swaying
but she was still shuddering,
so the lily pad shuddered, too.

"Be brave Little Frog," said Mama Frog.
"Most things that are scary are only just new.
You need to see what they are all about.
Listen to their voices.
Once you know them,
they aren't scary any more."

That was certainly puzzling.
Little Frog herself was pretty new,
and she wasn't scary.
But she always listened to Mama Frog.

So that day in early October,
Little Frog decided to try to be brave
and see what red and gold were all
about.
And orange.
She hopped back into the water—
the dark green water—
and began to swim.

Her heart was going *bumpity-bump*,
as she did the back stroke
and the side stroke,
and some frog-paddling, too.
But she made it to the shore.
Brave Little Frog.

She stuck one toe onto the brown dirt.
After green, Little Frog loved brown the best.
Brown is soft and comfortable and familiar.
She took one step, and another, and another,
though now her heart was going
bumpity-bump and *thumpity-thump*.
Brave, brave Little Frog.

Then Little Frog hopped a bit
down the twisty path
going toward the wood,
the wood that was so full of red and gold.
And orange.

She wasn't sure about orange.
Brave, brave, brave Little Frog.

Suddenly a wind whooshed through the trees.
Leaves began to rain down.
Red leaves.
Yellow leaves.
Orange leaves.
Scary leaves in scary colors,
making a scratchy-scratchy noise.
Little Frog hopped this way,

ran that way,

spun about,

fell down,

ran again.

She wasn't being very brave now.

By the time she stopped
hopping, running, spinning, and falling down,
Little Frog was lost.
Horribly,
   miserably,
      totally lost.

Besides, her right leg hurt.
There was a little scrape on her knee.
And a spot of red blood.
She shuddered again.
Suddenly she wasn't so sure about red.

It was dark in the woods,
except for those patches of red and gold.
And orange.
And purple as well.
She was *absolutely* not sure about purple.

Strange sounds came from everywhere.
Scary sounds.

Whirrrrr,
 Chirrrrr,
  Baroooooom,

Little Frog didn't feel very brave any more.
All she felt was scared.

But then Little Frog listened more closely
just as Mama Frog had told her to.

Whirrrrr,

That was the voice
of the wind through leaves.

Chirrrrr,

That was the voice
of a squirrel up a tree.

Baroooooom.

That was the voice
Papa Frog used in the spring.
All friendly sounds she knew.

But everything was strange indeed
because it wasn't spring,
it was autumn.
And autumn was scary.

Barooooooom,

Frightened all over again,
Little Frog looked for the sound.
And there, sitting on the top
of a huge pile of red and gold and orange
(and yes—even purple!) leaves
was Papa Frog himself
singing his spring song,
even though it was a scary autumn day.

"Come up, come up," sang Papa Frog.
"Think of the leaves as a lily pad."
Well, they didn't look like a lily pad.
They weren't the color of a lily pad.
But Little Frog tried to *imagine* them that way.

She climbed up the pile,
thinking *green, green, green*
all the way to the top,
even though the red and gold
and orange and purple leaves
were *scratchy-scratchy* underfoot.
Then she sat down by Papa Frog
right on top of the leaves
as if that pile was really a lily pad.

"There," boomed Papa Frog,
"that wasn't so bad, now, was it?"

For a while, Little Frog
thought about how bad it was.
Then she thought how the leaves
were actually crispy.
How they were gold like the rising sun,
orange like the sky at dawn,
and red like the sky at sunset.
She still wasn't sure about purple.

She thought about how autumn leaves
made a tickly sound in the wind.
They weren't scary at all, only new.
Papa Frog was right.
Mama Frog was right.
"Not *so* bad," she said to Papa Frog.
"Not the red and orange and gold," he said.
She noticed he didn't mention purple.

Then Little Frog and Papa Frog
slid down the pile together
with red and gold and orange
(and even purple) leaves
sliding down all around them.
It was so much fun,
Little Frog climbed up
and slid down again.
And again.
"Red and gold and orange
are not scary at all," said Little Frog.
"Not when you really get to know them."

Papa Frog looked at the pile again.
"And purple's not scary either," he said,
"only new."

At last, arm in arm,
Little Frog and Papa Frog
happily hopped and danced
all the way home to The Pond
where Mama Frog had made
a fresh shoo-fly pie for dinner,
something all three of them knew well.
It was still hot,
just the way they liked it best.
And even better,
inside it was all green.